This book belongs to:

_____

_____

_____

(Humphrey, please don't eat it!)

For Dan, erstwhile dancer and long-term friend

-Anna

To my dancing friends, I hope no blisters will ever stop
your dancing souls

- Laura

North Parade
Publishing Ltd
©2022 North Parade Publishing Ltd.
3-6 Henrietta Mews,
Bath BA2 6LR. UK
Printed in China.

Cinderella

as told by...

Humphrey Bookworm

Written by Anna Clothier

Illustrated by Laura Wood

Humphrey the bookworm is always **hungry.**

So hungry, in fact, that today he has eaten **two books,** a **newspaper, five letters,** *and* **Max's homework.**

And that was just for breakfast.

Last night, Humphrey told Max all about the

The Big Sad Wolf & The Mean Little Pigs

Now he knows what **really** happened, Max is determined to set the record straight.

He is taking Humphrey to school to tell his class that there are **two sides to every story**, and that they shouldn't believe everything they read about Big Bad Wolves.

Mum packs Max's lunchbox, and puts a leaflet in there for Humphrey.

Humphrey's **too small** to carry his own lunchbox, and besides, he hasn't got any arms.

Humphrey doesn't get the chance to eat his leaflet.

By lunchtime he has eaten **two textbooks,** **three spelling tests,** and a **poster.**

Mrs Miller says that Humphrey has to go home now, because he is eating her **register.**

Mum comes to collect Humphrey early, but he is still so exhausted from his day out that he won't tell any stories tonight.

Mum tells one instead.

It is all about **Cinderella**, her **two ugly sisters**, and a **handsome Prince** she meets at a ball.

"That isn't how it happened!" says Humphrey crossly, as Max carries him up to bed.

"Cinderella didn't have two ugly sisters; she had **two ugly blisters...**

...she went to a ball, and had **a fall...**

...and there was no Prince, just **Vince,** and he was a **landscape gardener.**"

"Why don't you tell me what **really happened?**" suggests Max, climbing into bed.

Humphrey clears his throat importantly.

*"**Once upon a time,**"* he begins,

"there lived a young woman who was very beautiful and very vain.

"She spent so long admiring herself in the mirror above the fireplace that the bottom of her dress became covered in cinders, and so she was called **'Cinderella'**.

"Cinderella was very fond of dancing, and attended **party** after **party** and **ball** after **ball.**

"She *whirled*, and *twirled*, and *sashayed*, and *swayed*, until, one day, **two angry blisters** appeared on the soles of her feet, and she could dance no more.

Cinderella was terribly upset. That night there was to be a grand ball at the Palace, but she couldn't possibly go. Try as she might, she could not cram her poor, swollen feet into her party shoes.

"The two **ugly blisters** throbbed and ached, and Cinderella wept bitterly.

"Just then, her **Fairy Godmother** appeared, clutching plasters and slippers."

"You mean **glass slippers!**" interrupts Max.

"No, I don't!" snaps Humphrey.

"This is what really happened..."

"'I'm not wearing **those!**' said Cinderella, eyeing the pink fluffy slippers with disgust.

"'Suit yourself!' snapped her Fairy Godmother. 'But you'll miss the ball, and **Vince Charming** is going to be there!'

"Cinderella swallowed her pride. She wore the **pink fluffy slippers**, and the plasters, but her feet were still **too sore to dance**.

"She did enjoy herself, though. She spent the evening chatting away to **Vince Charming**, who didn't seem to care about her slippers at all!

In fact, he rather liked them.

"Cinderella wanted to leave the party before anyone noticed her slippers.

"She had flip-flopped all the way out of the ballroom, and down the front steps, when **suddenly she stu**mbled, and fell.

"She landed in a heap on the Palace lawn, and, in an effort to hide her fluffy slippers, threw them into a hedge.

"Imagine Vince's surprise the next day when he came across Cinderella's slippers poking out from the box hedge he was pruning!

"He spread the word that as soon as he found the owner of the fluffy pink slippers, **he would marry her**.

"Alas, nobody at the ball had noticed anyone wearing slippers, and Cinderella was **too embarrassed** to admit that they belonged to her, though she dearly wanted to marry Vince.

"Soon **everyone** wanted a pair of fluffy slippers.

everyone else was *flip-flopping* about in the *brightest, fluffiest slippers* you can possibly imagine!

"In fact, Cinderella was the only person to wear party shoes to the next ball at the Palace;

"At last Cinderella was confident enough to tell Vince that the fluffy pink slippers belonged to her...

...and, of course, they married *and lived happily ever after.*"

"**So you see,**" says Humphrey, as he finishes his tale,

"**you don't always have to be like everybody else.**"

"**Good!**" says Max. "It would be ever so boring if we were all the same!"

"**Exactly!**" says Humphrey.

"But, Humphrey," yawns Max, as he settles down
to sleep, "what happened to all the books about
**Cinderella and Vince Charming, the
Landscape Gardener?**"

Humphrey looks sheepish.

"I ate them!" he says.